Up and Adam

By Debbie Zapata

Illustrated by Yong Ling Kang

KIDS CAN PRESS

Every morning

Up and Adam had a routine.

Adam got dressed.
Up made the bed.

Adam lined up cups, spoons and bowls, counting,
"One, two, three."

And Up's dog food always landed in
a perfect pile in the dish.

Today, Mom and Dad were huddled in front of the TV.

The news showed images of the big storm from last week.
Adam thought about that dark day. He and Up had hidden
as the wind whipped, thunder rumbled and rain poured.

A familiar voice came from the TV. It was
Madam Mayor.

"Good morning, Portville. I am happy to report that
the storm recovery is going well. But there is more
to do. By coming together and looking out for one
another, I know we can get there.

Now, it's time to get to work. *Up and at 'em!*"

BREAKING NEWS : PORTVILLE MAYOR PROVIDES UPDATE ON STORM RECOVERY

Did Madam Mayor just tell Up and Adam to get to work?
It sure sounded like it!

Adam turned to Up.

"We can help!"

Up jumped into the wagon, and they set off
to check on their favorite places.

Crack, crack, crack!
Sticks snapped under the wheels.

Adam said,
"We can help!"

They picked up big sticks and little sticks and added them to the pile. Up yipped and Adam hummed as they cleared the sidewalk.

When they were done, Adam smiled. Up smiled, too.

When they got to the school, Adam spotted Mr. Janitor.

Rattle, rattle, rattle!

He was cleaning up toys scattered by the storm.

Adam gave him a great big smile.
"Hi! Hiii!" he said.

"We can help!"

Adam parked the tricycles.
Up rolled the balls.

When they were done, Adam
smiled and waved goodbye.

Mr. Janitor smiled, too.

Then, like every day after school,
Up and Adam visited the park.

Tap, tap, tap!

A girl's hammer hit a nail on the head. She reached
into her pocket for another and came up empty.

Adam gave her a great big smile.
"Hi! Hiii!" he said.

"We can help!"

He grabbed some nails from
the toolbox and helped her
fix the birdhouse.

When they were done, Adam
smiled and clapped his hands.

The girl smiled, too.

Up and Adam dropped by their favorite pizzeria.

Sweep, sweep, sweep!

A boy's broom brushed dirt into a pile.

Adam gave him a great big smile.
"Hi! Hiii!" he said.

"We can help!"

Adam held the dustpan
and dumped the dirt.

When they were done, Adam
smiled and cheered.

The boy smiled, too.

The owner thanked them
with a slice of pizza.

She didn't forget Up.

Hmm, thought Adam.

Everyone loves a treat!

Up and Adam hurried home.

Adam turned on the oven. He lined up cookie sheets, rolls of dough and his favorite rocking cutter.

Beep, beep, beep!

The oven was ready.

Up and Adam baked batch after batch of
chocolate chip cookies and loaded the wagon.

They headed to the boardwalk,
Portville's favorite gathering place.

"Hi! Hiii!" Adam greeted each passerby with a cookie and his amazing smile.

Word spread.

More people came!

Some rode, others strolled and a few rolled up.

The line grew longer.

The laughter grew louder.

And the crowd grew cheerier.

Up and Adam handed out cookie after cookie.

Then a familiar voice came from the crowd.
It was Madam Mayor!

"Adam, your kindness has pulled Portville together.
Nice work!"

Adam smiled and gave her a high five.
Madam Mayor smiled, too.

When the cookies were gone,
Up and Adam waved goodbye
and headed home.

Every night Up and Adam had a routine.

Up yawned and stretched.

Adam lined up his toothpaste, toothbrush and rinse cup, counting, **"One, two, three."**

As Adam brushed his teeth,
he thought about the people
they had helped:

some big,
some small,
some worried,
and some holding out for hope.

When they saw Adam
smiling, they smiled, too.

That thought made Adam smile.

Then Adam looked in the mirror and
he saw that his smile made another smile.
And he realized …

*a pair of smiles
can make a difference.*

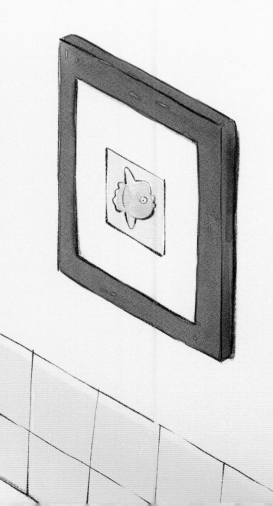

Up pulled back the covers.
Adam climbed into bed.

As they snuggled together, Adam smiled.
"We helped," he said.

Author's Note

When I had my first child, the doctor told me that my baby had trisomy 21, or Down syndrome. Down syndrome is a genetic condition in which a person has three copies of chromosome 21 instead of two. It is one of the most common chromosomal conditions in the world. While many people focused on what my son couldn't do, I concentrated on his strengths. My son Adam showed me that he is smart and strong.

At school, Adam is everyone's friend and he brightens people's days with his kind and loving heart. My son greets everyone with a cheery "Hi! Hiii!" He has a contagious smile, the best laugh, and fills the world around him with love. Everywhere he goes, Adam enriches people's lives. He reminds us to practice patience, share the gift of a smile and take time to have fun.

In the story, readers see how Up and Adam are part of their community and help in cleanup and recovery efforts. When the world chooses to include, it is a better place for everyone. People deserve to be treated with dignity and respect. To remove barriers and foster a more inclusive world, we need to start from childhood. When children socialize, they see similarities and accept people for who they are. Adults play an important role in creating opportunities to bring children together.

To learn more about Down syndrome and how you can be part of a movement of inclusion and acceptance, visit the resources listed on the next page.

— Debbie Zapata

Resources for Readers

GLOBAL

Best Buddies International is dedicated to establishing a global volunteer movement that creates opportunities for one-to-one friendships, integrated employment, leadership development and inclusive living for individuals with intellectual or developmental disabilities (IDD).

www.bestbuddies.org

Special Olympics believes that by playing and leading together, we are creating an inclusive and welcoming world for all. All over the world, Special Olympics is changing the lives of people with intellectual disabilities.

www.specialolympics.org

Global Down Syndrome Foundation is dedicated to significantly improving the lives of people with Down syndrome through research, medical care, education and advocacy. They work to educate governments, educational organizations and society in order to effect legislative and social changes so that every person with Down syndrome has a chance at a satisfying life.

www.globaldownsyndrome.org

CANADA

Best Buddies Canada helps to create lasting friendships between people with and without IDD. The ultimate goal is to make every school and community across Canada more inclusive and accepting of people with IDD.

www.bestbuddies.ca

The Canadian Down Syndrome Society focuses on human rights, health, social participation, inclusive education and employment for those with Down syndrome.

www.cdss.ca

Down Syndrome Resource Foundation empowers individuals with Down syndrome to reach their full potential throughout life by pioneering and providing educational programs and services, disseminating information and changing attitudes in Canada and beyond.

www.dsrf.org

THE UNITED STATES

The National Down Syndrome Society offers support to people with Down syndrome, their families, friends, teachers and coworkers, and educates the public about Down syndrome.

www.ndss.org

The National Down Syndrome Congress is dedicated to an improved world for individuals with Down syndrome. Their purpose is to promote the interests of people with Down syndrome and their families through advocacy, awareness and information.

www.ndsccenter.org

The Arc is dedicated to promoting and protecting the human rights of people with IDD and actively supporting their full inclusion and participation in the community throughout their lifetimes.

www.thearc.org

For Mama and Tata and my family. And for all individuals with disabilities and their families: keep lifting spirits with your smiles! — D.Z.

For Hui Ting. Your smile makes me happy! — Y.L.K.

Text © 2022 Debbie Zapata
Illustrations © 2022 Yong Ling Kang

Published in Canada and the U.S. by Kids Can Press Ltd.
25 Dockside Drive, Toronto, ON M5A 0B5

Kids Can Press is a Corus Entertainment Inc. company

www.kidscanpress.com

The artwork in this book was created using digital tools. The text is set in Berkeley Oldstyle.

Edited by Debbie Rogosin
Designed by Karen Powers

Printed and bound in Shenzhen, China, in 10/2021 by Imago.

CM 22 0 9 8 7 6 5 4 3 2 1

Library and Archives Canada Cataloguing in Publication

Title: Up and Adam / by Debbie Zapata; illustrated by Yong Ling Kang.

Names: Zapata, Debbie, author. | Kang, Yong Ling, illustrator.

Identifiers: Canadiana 20210226374 | ISBN 9781525304415 (hardcover)

Classification: LCC PZ7.1.Z37 Up 2022 | DDC j813/.6 — dc23

Kids Can Press gratefully acknowledges that the land on which our office is located is the traditional territory of many nations, including the Mississaugas of the Credit, the Anishnabeg, the Chippewa, the Haudenosaunee and the Wendat peoples, and is now home to many diverse First Nations, Inuit and Métis peoples.

We thank the Government of Ontario, through Ontario Creates; the Ontario Arts Council; the Canada Council for the Arts; and the Government of Canada for supporting our publishing activity.